SUKI
and the Magic Sand Dollar

SUKI
Silver Anniversary Edition

Suki and the Invisible Peacock
Suki and the Old Umbrella
Suki and the Magic Sand Dollar
Suki and the Wonder Star

Also by Joyce Blackburn

Sir Wilfred Grenfell: Doctor and Explorer

Theodore Roosevelt: Statesman and Naturalist

John Adams: Farmer from Braintree;
Champion of Independence

Martha Berry: A Woman of Courageous Spirit
and Bold Dreams

James Edward Oglethorpe

George Wythe of Williamsburg: Teacher of Jefferson
and Signer of the Declaration of Independence

The Earth Is the Lord's?

Roads to Reality

A Book of Praises

The Bloody Summer of 1742:
A Colonial Boy's Journal

Phoebe's Secret Diary:
Daily Life and First Romance
of a Colonial Girl, 1742

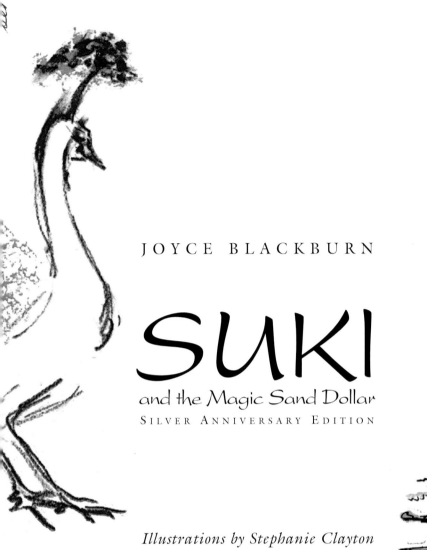

JOYCE BLACKBURN

SUKI
and the Magic Sand Dollar
SILVER ANNIVERSARY EDITION

Illustrations by Stephanie Clayton

PROVIDENCE HOUSE PUBLISHERS
Franklin, Tennessee

First edition 1969. Second edition 1996
Printed in the United States of America

00   99   98   97   96   5   4   3   2   1

Library of Congress Cataloging-in-Publication Data

Blackburn, Joyce.
    Suki and the magic sand dollar / Joyce Blackburn : illustrations by
Stephanie Clayton. — 2nd ed.
        p.   cm.
    Summary: When Suki visits Georgia's St. Simons Island with her family,
she makes new friends and learns many things about the sea.
    ISBN 1-881576-70-1
    [1. Seashore—Fiction. 2. Saint Simons Island (Ga.)—Fiction.
3.Friendship—Fiction. 4. Japanese Americans—Fiction.
5. Afro-Americans—Fiction.]
I. Clayton, Stephanie, ill. II. Title.
PZ7.B53223Sui   1996
[Fic]—dc20   96-14851
                                                               CIP
                                                               AC

Cover design by Schwalb Creative Communications Inc.

PROVIDENCE HOUSE PUBLISHERS
238 Seaboard Lane • Franklin, Tennessee 37067 • 800-321-5692

For
Elsie and Walter Goodwillie
Brenda and Renee

1

"Please fasten your seat belts and observe the No Smoking sign. We will be landing on St. Simons Island in approximately seven minutes." The voice, crisp and businesslike, came from a speaker right over Suki's head.

The big jet on which Suki had left Chicago that morning had been smooth and quiet. It had stayed above the clouds all the way to Atlanta. There, she had changed to this small "bluebird." That was the way she had thought of the plane during the ride south.

The "bluebird" flew low enough for her to watch its shadow touch the trees and fields and rivers and

houses on the ground. Suki could even see two boys crossing a bridge on their bicycles. For the first time she knew what people meant when they said they had "a bird's-eye view."

This was Suki's first flight. So that she could see outside as much as possible, Daddy had picked a seat next to the window for her. He and Mother sat in the row behind.

Suki's nose was cold from having pressed it against the window. That surprised her, because down there on the ground it was a warm summery day.

I'm glad my sisters chose to go to camp instead of coming along, Suki thought. *If Mari were here, she would be pointing and yelling, "Look at the water!" And Yuri, because she was the oldest, would act as though she knew everything. "We're landing on an island, Silly," she would say. "Islands are surrounded by water."*

Daddy almost always said sensible things. "That's the Atlantic Ocean to your left, Suki," he said.

He was taking pictures and Mother was studying a map of Georgia. Until one of their neighbors told them about it, they had never heard of St. Simons Island off the coast of Georgia. The "bluebird" shuddered with relief as its wheels dropped down into landing position.

"The Island looks like a buckwheat cake," Suki said.

"In shape maybe," Mother said. "But it's awfully green for a buckwheat cake, isn't it?"

The captain circled St. Simons Island so that the passengers could get a good look at it.

Now he was cutting back the speed—they were starting down easy. The *beep-beep* signal Suki liked was loud and regular. Down, down, down—over the water—the beach—the golf course—skimming the treetops and telephone cables—onto the runway.

The big tires squealed. The engines roared a final blast. The propellers sent gusts of wind, flattening the grass. The "bluebird" slowed, bumped to a standstill, then turned onto the strip leading to the little airport.

"Welcome to St. Simons Island," the stewardess said over the speaker. "Captain Bryant requests that you remain in your seats until we have come to a complete stop at the terminal gate. Have a perfect vacation, everyone!"

2

"Here, take my hand, Suki," Mother said as they walked from the plane.

Why does she act as though I'm a three year old, Suki thought, squinting into sunshine so bright she had to shade her eyes with her free hand.

A cluster of people waited under the airport awning.

"I have no idea what Mr. Goodwillie looks like," Daddy said.

"Well, he will certainly recognize *us*," Mother said.

"How can you be so sure when we haven't met?"

"We're the only *Nisei*," Mother replied. "There were no other Japanese-Americans on this plane."

"Of course!" Daddy laughed. "Either I'm stupid or you're smart." That sounded like a riddle to Suki. Other passengers were being met. She watched them hug and pound one another on the back as they shrilled names and hellos. It was suddenly noisier than her last birthday party.

Just as Daddy opened the airport door for her and Mother, a man called, "Mr. Gosho?"

"Yes," Daddy said. "Hello there. You must be Mr. Goodwillie."

"That's right." The two men shook hands.

Suki smiled at Mr. Goodwillie in his snowy white shirt and custard yellow slacks. He looked as cool as ice cream even though the sun was burning hot.

"Mr. Goodwillie, this is Mrs. Gosho," Daddy said. "And this is Suki."

"Welcome to our Island! Glad we have a pretty day for you folk. The station wagon is right around

the corner here—the white Fairlane. Why don't you three get in while I collect the bags?"

Mr. Goodwillie put on his dark glasses then opened the car door. Out bounced a medium-sized dog, panting and wagging her tail excitedly.

"Well, Brenda, are you glad to see the Goshos?" Mr. Goodwillie chuckled. "Don't jump up on Suki, you'll knock her over. Meeting planes makes Brenda forget her manners, I'm afraid."

Mother got into the station wagon, but Suki kneeled down to pat the bib of white under Brenda's chin. There was white on the tip of her tail, too, and on all four paws. The rest of her was brindle brown. The dog's rough tongue licked Suki's cheek, to tell her she was not a stranger.

"I'll help with those bags," Daddy said, following Mr. Goodwillie to the cart which pulled up and stopped nearby. It was piled high with hat boxes and suitcases and golf bags and packages.

In no time at all the luggage was loaded into the station wagon, and they were driving out of the parking lot onto a road lined with a tangle of green and leafy old trees. *Live oaks* Mr. Goodwillie called them. Their thick branches arched and touched overhead. To Suki the road was a "cozy" of shade, splashed here and there by dazzling light.

Her home in Chicago seemed far, far away. But Brenda the brown dog was close, her tail thumping merrily on the seat beside Suki.

13

3

"Here we are," Mr. Goodwillie announced, making a sharp turn to park behind a big white building.

"This is the Ship House, and we want you to enjoy your stay with us."

It did not take Brenda long to show Suki the entire motel, upstairs and down. No wonder it was called the Ship House. It was built to look like a ship. It even had a red-and-white-striped smokestack. And there were railings all around the porches. It reminded Suki of the steamer her family had taken last summer when they went across Lake Michigan.

But this was not a lake stretching into the distance as far as she could see. This was the ocean!

"I've never seen the ocean before," Suki said to Brenda. The dog did not hear—she was racing back and forth along the railing barking at the birds on the beach only a few yards away.

The ocean was bigger than any lake.

Suki could *feel* its bigness.

By suppertime the Goshos were settled comfortably in the spacious apartment upstairs with its floor-to-ceiling window which faced the water. While Mother was busy in the kitchen, Daddy and Suki looked up and down the beach and out to where the sky seemed to meet the ocean. How quiet it was.

"There are two sunsets, Daddy. One in the sky and one in the ocean."

"There won't be two for much longer," Daddy said. "Not with the tide changing. Those spits of sand away from shore where all the birds are waiting will soon be covered by water, and a breeze will ruffle the mirror that reflects the sunset. The beach, all the way to the dunes, will be covered."

"How high will the water come?" Suki asked. She was not scared. At least, she did not think she was.

"Not past the rock wall in front of the Ship House," Daddy said. "By midnight you'll hear the waves rolling in—that is, if you're awake."

"Let's not put any ideas into small heads," Mother called from the kitchen.

Quickly Daddy added, "Of course, you won't be awake, Suki. You'll be sound asleep when the tide comes in."

"When will it be low again the way it is now, Daddy?"

"In twelve hours and twenty-five minutes."

"How can you tell?"

"Because, Suki, along this part of the Atlantic coast, it takes that long for one high tide to go out and the next to come in."

"It never changes?"

"Never."

"Then tides are clocks!"

"Yes, you might call them clocks. They keep time the way the sunrise and sunset do—the way the seasons do."

"How, Daddy?"

Daddy took off his glasses and began polishing

them with a clean handkerchief before replying.

"That's a big question, Suki. If I were a scientist, I could explain better. I just know that nature has rules or patterns that we can depend on. In our part of the world tides rise and fall on schedule, the sun and moon rise and set on schedule, the seasons come in succession—summer follows winter. These laws of nature keep our world in order. Can you imagine how it would be without them?"

Suki thought for a moment. "All mixed up," she said.

"Mixed up! That's what I am in this strange kitchen," Mother exclaimed. "The biscuits are hard as bricks. But if you two can tear yourselves away from that window. . . ."

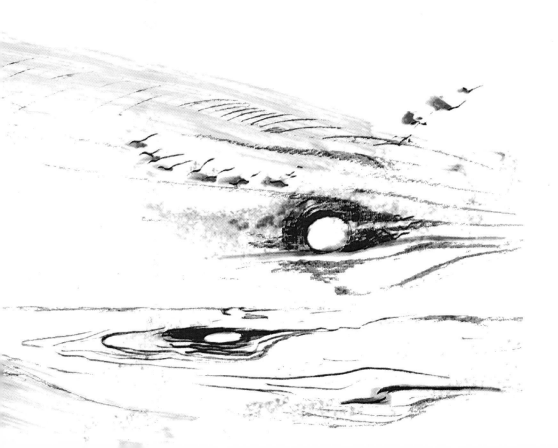

4

Suki tried her best to stay awake till midnight when the tide would come in.

What made it come and go?

Where had it been?

On a map of the world, Daddy had pinpointed St. Simons Island. Of course, it was too small to show, but across the Atlantic from St. Simons was the Rock of Gibraltar.

My, that's miles and miles, Suki thought. *If I followed the tide, would it take me all that way?*

Suki did not find out. Before she and the tide had gone very far, it had rocked her to sleep.

When she awakened, sunshine was slanting across
the foot of her bed, and a cool wet nose was nudging
her elbow. Brenda! Her front paws on the pillow, she
wagged her tail wildly and gave Suki a look which
plainly said, *Get up! Hurry! We have lots of exploring
to do!*

Suki could hear voices nearby as the dog almost
pushed her into the bathroom. Looking at her face
in the mirror, she said, "I might go swimming,
Brenda, so there doesn't seem much point in
washing my ears. My teeth can wait. No, Mother is
sure to ask if I brushed them."

Suki had trouble finding the buttons on the back
of her sunsuit, she was in such a hurry and was so
eager to run on the beach with the dog.

"All thumbs!" she fussed. "There! Now we can go, Brenda. We will just have time for breakfast."

The voices she had heard belonged to Mother and Daddy and a woman with a cheery smile.

"This must be Suki," the woman said. "I'm Mrs. Goodwillie."

"How do you do?" Suki said, the way Mother wanted her to do.

"Mrs. Goodwillie brought you something," Mother said.

"Something to eat?" Suki was suddenly hungry.

"No, I'm afraid not," Mrs. Goodwillie laughed.

"We thought you might like to use our book on seashells while you're here."

"Oh, thank you, Mrs. Goodwillie." On the jacket of the book was a beautiful photograph of a shell.

"That's a conch."

Mrs. Goodwillie laughed again. "Well, maybe *you* don't need the book."

"It's the only shell I know," Suki said. "I drew one in Art class once, and Miss Kelly gave me an A on it."

"You'll find lots of shells to draw before you leave. And speaking of leaving, I'd better do something besides stand here and talk. See you later."

Mrs. Goodwillie left behind her a kind of music that vibrated in the air, the way the sound of a sweet wind chime does. Brenda stayed for breakfast. Suki gulped hers when Mother was not looking.

5

The sand was hot except at the water's edge. The wind blew tiny grains of it from the dunes. They prickled her face.

The ocean's foamy ripples lapped back and forth, back and forth over Suki's toes. She could feel the sand being sucked from under her.

She had permission from Mother to walk all the way to the big white Coast Guard station with Brenda, but the dog was racing ahead into the distance. Suki suddenly did not want to follow. Just standing there, looking—feeling—listening was enough.

Green and blue—water and sky—she was part of them. A bird darted over her toes. She would not have known it was a bird from the touch, but she was watching bubbles collect on her feet. The bird was almost invisible; its pale coloring blended with the wet sand. On spindly black legs it ran just ahead of the wash of the waves, calling *peep-peep.* With its sharp bill it probed for food. No sooner did she see it than a whole flock appeared from nowhere. They moved together in perfect unison. Suki thought some unseen drill master must be saying,

ONE—TWO—THREE—Advance and probe.
ONE—TWO—THREE—Retreat and wait.

She did not know how long she watched the sandpipers feed before she noticed the water was deepening. The tide was rising around her. I'd better find a dry spot and sit down, she decided. I want to see what the birds do next.

22

The drill master must have signaled at that very moment, because they rose gracefully and turned on the wing, their white breasts twinkling in the sunlight, the sea green behind them. With military precision they landed on the sand near Suki, lined up in even rows as though they had practiced and practiced. There were six rows once they stopped shifting positions. Three to seven "peeps" in each, thirty-four all together. She counted them.

Another funny thing—the birds each stood on one leg and faced into the wind. To Suki they looked like a regiment of wounded soldiers; she felt sorry for them. That is, until they turned their heads to the right and tucked their bills under their back feathers. They were going to take a nap!

Before Suki could guess what their next maneuver would be, she heard a friendly bark. Brenda came bounding toward her. Beside the dog, running in long easy strides, was a lady wearing a big green hat. Suki had never seen such a large hat.

As the lady with the big hat came nearer and nearer, Suki saw that the dark face under the floppy brim was laughing. The dog was laughing too. They both arrived panting at Suki's side and tumbled down in a heap onto the sand.

"Hi!" the lady said. "That Brenda beats me every time. Whew!" She was out of breath. Still her voice was low and full of chuckles when she asked Suki, "What's your name?"

"Suki Gosho. What's yours?"

"Cherry. Cherry Hunter."

Suki did not feel shy. They smiled at each other. Cherry's teeth were pearly and even.

"Where do you stay, Cherry?"

"A few blocks that way toward the village."

"We're at the Ship House."

"*That's* how Brenda knew you. She wouldn't give up until I came here to meet you." Cherry took off the big hat and fanned herself. "Where are you from, Suki?"

"Chicago, Illinois."

"Chicago. I was there for a meeting at the University a few months ago. I live in Washington, D.C. That's a big city too."

"What do you do in Washington? Do you work for the president of the United States?"

24

"Well, in a way I guess I do. In a way I also work for you. I've been assigned to a government project on water pollution. But I'm just an ordinary scientist."

Suki had never met a scientist before.

"I asked my daddy about tides, and he said if he were a scientist he could tell me more about them. Do you know about tides?"

"Not much, really. The oceans cover three-fourths of the earth's surface. That's a lot of water. And it is all affected by the sun and the moon even though they are hundreds of thousands of miles away. Let's say this is our earth." Cherry drew a circle in the sand.

"Here's the sun. During the day it pulls the oceans toward it. But the moon is closer to earth than the sun." She drew the moon.

"The moon's pull is stronger. As the earth turns, and the moon moves around it, the tides follow it. Here on St. Simons Island every twelve hours and twenty-five minutes the tide rises to its highest stage, because the water flows toward the land. Then it flows back. When it flows back, we say it is *ebb tide*."

"The way it was at breakfast time?"

"Yes. See how it's rising now? Since we've been sitting here? By 2:30 this afternoon water will cover this place. The tide will be high. Then around 9:00 tonight, it will be ebb tide again."

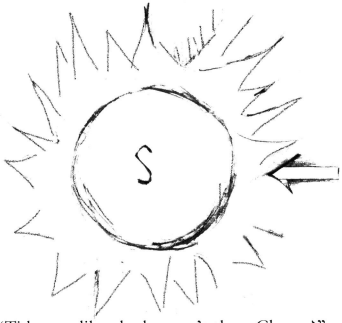

"Tides are like clocks aren't they, Cherry?"

"That's a good way to think of them—nature's clocks—clocks that never run down!"

"Who started them?"

"Well, Suki, some scientists call Him Super-Mind. I call Him God. Others whom I know don't believe there is anyone behind the fantastic laws that keep our universe from flying to pieces. But one thing is certain, no scientist has ever made or created such a law. We only discover nature's laws. Some genius set them in motion, made them up, and I'm convinced this Maker keeps them regulated."

"What if he didn't?"

"Well, for instance, if the pattern the moon follows changed tonight and let it come closer to earth, the tides would be high enough to cover this Island. Both coastlines of the United States could disappear beneath the sea. But we know that's not going to happen. The moon stays in its place—in the very orbit which was designed for it.

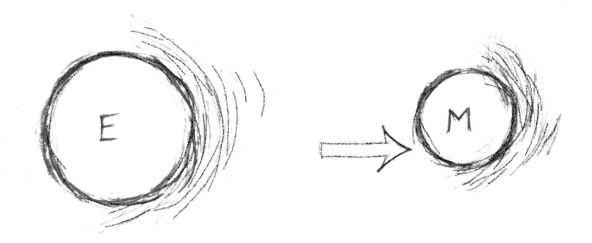

Every created thing has a law or design built into it, and *I* can't imagine any better name for the Designer than God."

They talked and talked until Cherry took Suki by the hand and pulled her to her feet.

"Take a deep breath, Suki. Another one. Isn't the salt air heavenly? If you're around tomorrow, maybe we can discover more clocks."

Cherry squashed the big floppy hat down over her high forehead.

"I don't want you to go," Suki said.

"And I wish I could stay, but my sister needs a baby-sitter."

Suki had to skip to keep up with Cherry on their way up the beach. Brenda was nowhere to be seen.

"Your lunch will be ready soon," Cherry said and gave Suki's cheek a little pinch. "See you again, and don't let the tide carry you off!" She turned up the path that led from the Ship House yard to the street, her low laugh drifting behind her.

6

"Your milkshake is in the refrigerator, Suki," Mother called a few minutes later.

Suki liked to drink through a straw. She took the shake along and went to see what was going on outside the big window where her parents were sunning on the deck.

"What are you doing?" she asked.

"Not a thing," Mother yawned lazily. It was one of the few times Suki had seen her mother doing *not a thing*. Back home there was the gift shop to tend, Daddy to take care of, *and* three little girls. Suki thought of the time she had overheard her mother say, "Work, work, work—I'll be glad when the girls are old enough to help more." Her voice had been tired and cross. Suki promised herself she would never again try to get out of work at home. She would stop pretending to practice the piano every time she was supposed to help with dishes.

"I'm watching pelicans," Daddy said, bringing her back to the present. "Here, Suki, take a look. They're fishing now that the tide is coming in."

Suki adjusted the binoculars. It was always fun when Daddy let her look through them.

There went a long straight line of pelicans, their wings barely clearing the waves. The leader sailed, then *flapped-flapped* his wings and sailed again. Each bird behind him did the same thing.

"You should have seen them earlier, Suki, when they were standing on the sandbar. They looked very old and solemn. Their wingspread is wider than I can stretch my arms!"

"Oh, oh, the lead pilot must have spotted a fish," Suki said. "He's turning and going higher—see, Daddy?"

"Twenty-five feet into the air at least."

"What's he going to do?"

"Just watch, dear, and don't ask so many questions."

The weird brown pelican pulled its head close to its body, partly closed its great wings, then plunged down, down. Suki could imagine its great pouch snapping shut under the waves. When the bird surfaced, it pointed its closed bill downward to drain out the water scooped up by the great pouch. But in an instant, it pointed the bill upward and opened it with an awkward gulp.

"He's swallowing something!" Suki cried. "Look, the other pelicans are going for fish too. Don't they make a big splash?"

"The way you do when you dive," Daddy teased. "Like a rock. May I borrow the glasses a minute, Suki? A smaller customer seems to be joining the fun. Yes sir, a gull, and you two won't believe it, but that gull is lighting right on a pelican's back. He's not going to miss any leftovers."

Daddy laughed until Mother and Suki took turns looking through the glasses and laughed too. Suki could not remember when they had laughed this much together. So many things were happening out over the water for them to watch: flashy black skimmers with bright red legs and forked tails fished gracefully, making faint complaining sounds while the terns shrieked wildly above them. Terns were the birds that zoomed high against the sky, wheeled, and plummeted, as deadly as jet fighters, to spear their prey.

When the shrimp trawlers began appearing over the horizon, flocks of terns hovered and dived in the wakes of the boats. All the way into dock they performed breathtaking acrobatics.

Off to the north, there were boys on surfboards, who, bird-like, rode the crests of the breakers. Faster

and faster the waves shot them toward shore till
the boys fell sideways into the froth—out of sight,
    bobbed up,
        shook their heads,
            and waved triumphantly.
    The tide was high. Movement stirred the sea
everywhere.
    Suki could feel it in the air as she watched spray
collect in crystal beads on her shoulders and trickle
down her arms leaving flakes of salty glitter.

7

Not a day of the Island vacation passed that Suki did not make a new discovery. The pockets of her clothes stayed wet. They bulged with shells, sponges, pieces of colored glass, and rusty bolts that poked holes in the corners of her pockets. *Back home Mother always wants me to look so-so*, Suki thought. *But here she doesn't care. Another thing about "here" is that she laughs a lot. And she doesn't bustle.*

"See, Mother, the shell I found?"

"What under the sun is it, dear? See if it's in the shell book, why don't you?"

"Cherry will know, Mother."

"Who is Cherry? Is she the grown-up I saw you talking with on the beach?"

Mother took off her dark glasses, sat up straight in the deck chair, and motioned for Suki to sit at her feet. This was surely more fun than just watching from the Ship House window.

"Cherry is my new friend," Suki said. "She's a scientist. A real scientist. She knows everything."

"Oh? As much as Best Friend?"

The Invisible Peacock—haven't thought of him for days, Suki realized with a start. *Funny, Mother didn't seem to be kidding the way she usually did about Best Friend. Just because he was invisible didn't keep him from being real. Maybe Mother had caught on at last.*

Suki remembered the very first time she and the Invisible Peacock had met. It was on a busy street corner. He had escaped from a Chicago zoo and was about to starve. She had talked him into living in the Paradise tree outside the window of her room.

Almost from the beginning she had called him Best Friend, because she could tell him anything—the most secret things. For a while they did everything together. But that was when she was very young.

"Mother, do you know why I didn't bring Best Friend along?"

"No, Suki, why?"

"Because I've grown up!"

Mother smiled. "Two years do make a difference, but we never forget the happy times we've had with our invisible playmates."

She said that as though she had also had a playmate you couldn't see, Suki suddenly realized. *After all Mother had been a little girl once upon a time.*

"Maybe you would like to invite Cherry to lunch tomorrow, then Daddy and I can meet a real scientist too."

"Oh, that would be perfect, Mother. She'll be here any minute. I'll ask her first thing."

Suki ran to the deck railing and looked up the beach. Was that Cherry clambering over the steep wall of jagged rocks? Yes, that was the big green hat.

She could see Brenda, too, jumping from one rock to another, leading the way.

"They're coming right now, Mother. We want Brenda for lunch along with Cherry, don't we?"

"Of course, dear, if she likes shrimp salad."

Suki hurried down the Ship House steps and ran to meet her friends.

"Look, Cherry, what I found," she said, holding high her treasure.

"The shell of a horseshoe crab, and it isn't broken!" Cherry took it from Suki's hands carefully. "This is the season for them." She turned it over.

"Wonder what happened to the fellow who lived in here?"

The shell was a shiny leathery brown, the color of Cherry's skin.

"Isn't this some hinge attaching the tail part to the large front shield, Suki? Works, too, see?"

"Let me try it," Suki said. "He must not have been very old, because his hinge doesn't squeak."

"Maybe he kept it oiled," Cherry laughed. "Horseshoe crabs come from a family older than dinosaurs, Suki. And they have built-in clocks, as you say."

"What do you mean?" Suki asked.

"*Only* at this time of year and *only* when the moon is brightest do horseshoe crabs crawl from the bottom of the ocean onto shore. They come in pairs when the tide is high. *Only* when it is high."

"Do a lot of them come, Cherry?"

"I've seen them come by the hundreds. I suspect this shell belonged to a male horseshoe crab. The males are smaller than the females. I wish you could have seen his feet."

"Why?"

"Because they're made a special way so that he can hang onto the female when she drags him onto the beach with her."

"Why does she do that?"

"So that he will be on hand to fertilize the thousands of eggs she lays. . . . "

"Thousands?" Suki interrupted.

"Yes, thousands. Then after the eggs are laid in the nest of sand and fertilized, the couple starts back to the water as the tide begins to go out. From the crab trails I've examined, I think they must lose their way sometimes. If they don't get back to the ocean by daybreak, the heat from the sun can kill them. Or a gull can come along, flip Mr. Horseshoe over on his back and have fresh crab. In which case, this is all there is left."

"But that's murder!" Suki protested.

"Pretty bad if you're a crab! But that isn't the

end of the drama," Cherry went on. "Don't forget the eggs in the sand. In two weeks they'll be ready to hatch, and again, the high tide helps."

"How?"

"By churning the sand around the mother crab's nest. You know how sandpaper cuts and smooths soft wood?"

"Yes."

"Well, the sand cuts the membrane covering the eggs until it splits open and lets the baby crabs out. In a short time they develop tails and take off for the floor of the sea where they grow and grow. In nine or ten years they're ready to reproduce the exact way their parents did, and on the very same schedule."

"Really and truly, Cherry?" Suki's eyes were round with wonder.

"I wouldn't be surprised, Suki, if every single living cell, whether in plants or animals, whether on the land or in the ocean, has a built-in clock."

Cherry shed her jacket suddenly and dropped the big hat on top of it. "*My* clock says it's time to take a swim!"

Without another word she waded into the surf until it was deep enough for her to dive and caper with the grace of a dolphin.

Suki wished she could go in too, but she had promised not to. Daddy had said she could play on the beach all she liked so long as she promised to go swimming only when he was with her. At that very moment the promise seemed unfair. (Even Brenda could go with Cherry!) But she and Daddy had never broken a promise to each other. Maybe he would be back from playing golf with Mr. Goodwillie. Then he would swim with her the way he had the other afternoons.

No sooner had Suki built a sand castle with lots of tunnels and turrets than Brenda changed course and started back to shore. The closer she came, the louder she barked.

Get ready! Here I come! she seemed to be barking.

Right into the middle of the sand castle Brenda charged and shook a great shower of sea water all over Suki.

"Brenda! Shame on you, look at what you've done to me! And look at my sand castle!" Suki scolded. "Why didn't you stay in the water—*you* don't have to get permission to swim the way some people do."

The brindle dog cocked her ears and listened to Suki, but she was not discouraged. Her long tail

38

switching back and forth with delight, she licked Suki's chin lovingly as if to say: *But I want to be with you.*

"You'll have to sit down then and stop getting in my way," Suki said, pushing the dog into a sitting position. "It sure is hot. Why don't you bring me Cherry's big hat?"

Brenda walked to the hat, picked it up, the brim between her teeth, and dragged it over to Suki. "You're not a dog, Brenda," Suki gasped in surprise. "You're people!"

Just as she said that, a muffled rumble sounded out over the ocean. Suki was not sure it was thunder, but Brenda was. The dog's tail stopped wagging abruptly to droop between her legs and she headed lickety-split for the Ship House.

At the same time Cherry, with even quick strokes, started swimming back to the beach. Suki, almost hidden by the big hat, stood and waved to her.

"Looks like a storm coming," Cherry said as she ran up, breathless from her swim. "I get an afternoon off from baby-sitting, and it rains." She laughed and wrapped the jacket around her. "Say, that hat suits you to a T." She took a mirror from her pocket and held it for Suki to see herself. Suki made a funny face.

"It's better than an umbrella, Cherry."

"Well, hold on to it, and let's get you home. Come on, I'll race you back to the Ship House."

It was a good thing they did not have far to go, because Suki could not keep the hat on and run fast too.

They reached the Ship House porch just as a great bare tree of lightning branched across the sky. It seemed to be a signal to the thunder, which crackled, and to the wind, which began to blow so hard it made Suki shut her eyes tight. When she opened them again, a sullen roily cloud hid the white ball of sun, as though it were a window blind jerked down on the horizon.

"You'd better stay here with me until the storm is over, Cherry."

"That would be fun, but I can't."

"You'll get wet. It's starting to rain," Suki said.

Cherry grinned. "I had a swim, remember? I'm already soaked. I must get a shower and be dressed when my sister brings Renee back from the dentist."

"Who's Renee?"

"My favorite niece," Cherry said. "You'll have to meet her."

For a moment Suki wished there was no one named Renee. *She* must be the reason Cherry was always hurrying off.

"Mother told me to invite you for lunch tomorrow, Cherry. I almost forgot."

"I'd love that, Suki. What time?"

"About twelve-thirty."

"Fine," Cherry said, jumping from the porch to

the ground. "Bye! Don't let the wind blow you away." She ran up the path to the street.

"Wait, you forgot your hat," Suki called.

"You keep it for me," Cherry yelled over her shoulder.

That was when the rain began coming down in sheets. The drops were so huge, and they fell so thick and fast, Suki could not see Cherry at all.

But she would be back tomorrow for lunch.

8

Suki was glad Mother decided to have the lunch
for Cherry outside on the deck. It was breezy and
sunny—there was not a cloud in the blue, blue sky.

She had washed the lettuce for the salad while
Mother cleaned the shrimp. Daddy made his special
dressing. He asked her to taste it several times.
"Enough green onions, Suki?"

"Just right, Daddy."

When Cherry arrived, everything was ready. Suki
passed around the coral-colored napkins that
matched the trays. It was more like a party, eating
from trays on their laps.

The grown-ups were soon talking as though they
had known one another for a long time. Suki did not

mind listening—they were talking about her—but she wished for a friend her own age who would talk *to her.*

She heard Cherry say, "Your Suki has enough curiosity for twins, Mr. Gosho."

Daddy raised his eyebrows and shook his head. "More than we can satisfy," he said. "We're thankful you came along to answer her questions. Mother and I are short on scientific facts, I'm afraid."

"Well, I suspect facts may not be as important as we adults make them, Mr. Gosho," Cherry said. "The other day a wave knocked Suki down. She hopped up laughing and told me the wave looked like a twist of green taffy. She told me how salty it tasted and how it 'bumped' the breath out of her. She made me envious, because that same wave added up to just so many figures to me. How fast was it traveling? How high was it when it crested? How much force was in it per square foot? I was learning *about* it, not *from* it," Cherry chuckled as though she had told a joke on herself.

Daddy chuckled too. "I believe it was the American, Thoreau, who said a man has not seen a thing until he has felt it. He might say you were testing the wave instead of tasting it."

"Exactly, Mr. Gosho."

That was the Invisible Peacock's word, "exactly." Suki suddenly missed him more than she

had all vacation. And before she knew it, she was
thinking about Best Friend instead of listening to the
talk which was way over her head anyway. She did
not know how long it was until Cherry said
something which caught her attention again, "The
moon will be full tomorrow night, and I've promised
to take my niece, Renee, hunting for turtles. This is
when they come up on the beach to lay eggs, and
I've spotted three crawls—trails—near the dune
north of here. Would you like to come with us?"

"How about it, Suki?" Daddy asked. "Would you like that?"

"Oh, yes, Daddy. Will we get to stay up late?"

"That depends on what Mother says."

"Oh, Mother, say yes—please, please."

"Let's say it depends on the turtles," Mother said, pretending to be serious. "We won't want to miss them even if they're late, will we?"

Suki hugged her mother and cried, "Oh, I can hardly wait!"

9

The night was warm and friendly.

From a saffron bow on the horizon, the moon had blossomed into a perfect sphere.

Up, up it rode the sky, pouring silver across the water and the deserted beach.

Suki could feel the moon smiling. She could see it reflected small and far away in Daddy's glasses. It turned Mother's shirt white-white and Cherry's face black-black. It cast a pair of shadows alongside her and Renee. The big hat spooked them.

Loud voices and mewing gulls and ships' whistles belonged to the day. There was a hush that belonged to the night. The hush was inside Suki, and it was everywhere outside her, a part of the moonlight.

She almost whispered as she and Renee ran toward the high finger of land that pointed into the sea. That was where they were headed.

"I wish Cherry had brought you along sooner," Suki said. When Cherry and her niece had arrived for what they called the "turtle patrol," Suki forgot the mean thought that had popped into her head the first time she had heard the name Renee. Why, they were the same age and in the same grade! They were even the same height—3'7" tall.

"Our vacation lasts only one more day and night." Suki said dejectedly. "Oh, Renee, I do wish you had come with Cherry days and days ago!"

"So do I," Renee said.

The pair of shadows slowed to a walk. "We're a long way from the Ship House, aren't we, Suki?"

"Yes, turn around and look at it. It's a ghost ship drifting on the dark," Suki answered dreamily, but a shiver chased up her backbone an instant later when something rattled the clump of sea oats they were passing. "What was that, Renee?"

"A raccoon probably," Renee said calmly. "He's looking for turtles too."

"Why?"

"He wants to know where they hide their eggs. He won't hurt you."

Suki was glad when the grown-ups caught up. "Can you believe it's after midnight?" her daddy asked. She had never been up this late.

"The tide is almost high," Cherry said. "And here's the turtle crawl I found this morning. Renee, you and Suki walked right over it!"

The moonlight revealed a yard-wide track, as though a heavy flat object had been dragged through the sand. To the sides of the track were patterns made by the turtle's flippers, and its tail had left little sharp marks down the middle.

"Mother Turtle was here all right looking for a good nesting place, but she didn't lay any eggs," Cherry said. "We'll pick a spot near the high-water mark and wait in case she comes back to finish the job."

"For how long?" Suki asked.

"How long can you sit still? It may be for ten minutes—it may be two hours. *If* she comes."

They all sat down on the slope of a dune—Suki on one side of Cherry—Renee on the other. Daddy put his arm around Mother, and they leaned their heads together.

"We heard a raccoon, Aunt Cherry," Renee said.

"Oh, oh, an enemy spy. See if you two can be as quiet as he is. If we frighten Mother Turtle as she comes out of the ocean, she'll turn around and swim away. But if we don't make any noise till she starts working on her nest, then she'll let us get close enough to watch."

The surf is coming nearer, Suki mused. *I wonder if that sneaky raccoon is watching us.* A million thoughts idled in her head as minutes ticked into hours. At least her bottom felt as though they had waited for hours. The sand that had seemed soft and silky was really hard and damp. Besides, her legs ached. She wished she could stretch and turn cartwheels.

Suddenly, Cherry was pointing. At first, Suki could not see anything. Yes, yes, she could just make out a large, blackish object riding a wave up the beach not more than twenty feet away. It was Mother Turtle!

The turtle looked around and took a *breather.* Then, rested, she began her lumbersome crawl towards the dunes out of reach of the high tide. Lifting and shoving, her flippers could only move her four-foot-long body over the sand an inch at a time.

There! That place suited her. With first one hind flipper, then the other, she began to dig a nest. Her flippers were like small shovels or scoops.

"Now, we can get as close to her as we want," Cherry said, leading the "turtle patrol" over to the nest site.

DIG—DIG—DIG—SCOOP—SCOOP—SCOOOOP—

Pile the sand—Pile it carefully to one side.

Rest that flipper.

DIG—DIG—DIG—SCOOP—SCOOP—SCOOOOP—

Pile the sand high.

Rest the other flipper.

No bulldozer could have been more efficient.

The final step was to scatter the pile of sand and push hard against the sides of the nest to pack it.

DIG—SCOOP—PILE—SCATTER—PACK

Again and again the turtle repeated the steps, almost as though she were doing a slow, stately dance.

"It's going to be a big hole, isn't it, Cherry?" Suki whispered.

"Yes, and notice, it will be larger at the bottom than at the top. You can see the circular shape of it now."

The ancient ritual held the watchers spellbound until the turtle finally stopped to rest.

"The hole is two feet deep," Daddy estimated. "She must be about ready to lay her eggs."

"She is getting into position," Cherry agreed.

"Watch closely, Suki, Renee. She'll move her front flippers a bit each time she drops an egg. If you count, you'll know how many eggs she lays."

Suki and Renee, eager to begin, squatted in front of Mother Turtle.

One, two, three, four, five, six, seven . . . ten . . . nineteen . . . twenty-five, twenty-six . . . thirty . . . forty, forty-one, forty-two, forty-three. . . .

"She's crying!" Suki exclaimed. "Look at the big tears, Cherry. Oh, dear, now I've lost count."

"Sixty" . . . Renee said to help Suki get back in the game.

Sixty-seven . . . seventy. . . eighty. . . ninety. . . one hundred . . . one hundred and one . . . one hundred and two . . . one hundred and three . . . one hundred and four. . . .

Suki waited, not daring to breathe. Was the turtle stopping? Time stood still. Yes, it was all over.

"One hundred and four!" Suki and Renee sang out as the turtle rested. "One hundred and four eggs!"

But Mother Turtle's work was not finished. In a few minutes she began shoveling sand over the nest of eggs with her hind flippers. She packed it down and scattered it for twelve feet in all directions. When she stopped it was certainly hard to tell exactly where the nest was.

Her work done, it was time for the turtle to start back to the water. She was so tired she could barely drag her great bulk in the right direction. She did not even make the effort to lift her tail. It left an unbroken furrow in the crawl behind her. After many, many rest stops, at last she reached the water's edge. Almost an hour had passed since she began her work.

The surf lifted her slightly, and she looked slowly up and down the shore as though she was sorry to leave the precious eggs behind. Then with head raised high and proud, she used her last ounce of energy to catch the next wave. It floated her off the beach—out, out, out to the deep.

"Now she can rest," Cherry sighed.

The moonlight was as bright as ever, but they could no longer see Mother Turtle.

"Where has she gone?" Suki wondered aloud.

"Yes, where is she?" Renee echoed.

"No one knows," Cherry said.

Nothing more was said. The five friends walked toward the Ship House. The shore was quiet and Suki was sleepy. She was glad Renee and Cherry had agreed to stay the rest of the night with her and Mother and Daddy—the "turtle patrol."

10

Suki might have slept all of the next morning if the smell of bacon and toast had not teased her awake. She hurriedly bathed and dressed.

When she came to the breakfast table, she rubbed her eyes and looked around the circle of faces, smiling. It was too soon to talk about the night's adventure. They listened to the saucy perking of the coffeepot instead.

"How about checking the turtle nest before Renee and I go home?" Cherry asked when they were finished eating.

"Oh, let's," Suki said.

How different the beach looked. Fog drifted off the water, velvety and gray. The ocean was one vast blur—the sun was invisible except for veins of yellow here and there. Suki and Renee tried to keep up with Cherry. A funny suspense propelled them. "It will take two months for the baby turtles to hatch," Cherry said. "Lots can happen in two months."

"Like what?" Suki wanted to know.

"Any number of things, unfortunately. Ghost crabs often tunnel under the nest and ruin the eggs which they can feast on the rest of the summer. You already know raccoons are a real threat. Sometimes they are so bold they grab the eggs as they're being laid! Worse than that, two-legged animals steal turtle eggs."

"People you mean?"

"Yes, people. If they get caught, they're fined, but they still go on robbing nests."

A cold dread gripped Suki as they came to the patch of scattered sand which camouflaged the nest. Tracks, shaped like tiny hands, covered the site. Shattered eggshells lay strewn all around, some of the yolks still wet and orange on the sand. Big green flies buzzed in greedy clusters on the remains, but the spying raccoon had been there first!

"I was afraid this would happen," Cherry said. "He must have dug up the eggs as soon as we were out of sight."

A lump seemed stuck in Suki's throat. She was afraid she was going to cry. And to make matters worse, Cherry said, "Well, Renee, your mother will think we've run off to Timbuktu. We'd better be on our way."

Cherry walked back down the beach so fast it was as though she were angry. Suki and Renee ran beside her. When they came to the path which turned out to the street, Cherry stopped and leaned down so that she could look straight into Suki's eyes. "When things go wrong my people sing," she said. "It always helps." And she began to sing in her low, dark voice:

> O bring me a 'gator
> O gal when you come off the islan'—
> A ring-tail 'gator
> O gal when you come off the islan'—

"My great-grandfather taught me that when I was a little girl, Suki. Long ago, on this very island, he had been a slave. Life was very hard, but he had songs for the bad times as well as songs for the good times, and he gave them to me."

"Aunt Cherry, let's give this one to Suki," Renee said.

"Let's do!"

They began to sing again and Suki hummed along. She knew the tune already. Singing it did help when Renee and Cherry left her alone on the path.

All of the rest of that day she sang the song. Still she was sad. Not only about the turtle eggs. Tomorrow would be her last day on St. Simons. When she didn't eat her lunch, Mother asked, "Don't you feel well, Suki?" How she hated questions.

When she did not go down to the beach to play, Brenda came looking for her. The dog knew something was wrong. She squeezed between Suki's ankles and looked up with a puzzled expression.

When Suki did not put on her bathing suit for their usual swim before supper, Daddy said, "Something bothering you, Suki?"

Suki shook her head, but two fat tears rolled down her cheeks.

"Won't you tell me what's wrong?"

"The raccoon ate all the turtle eggs, Daddy."

Daddy pulled her close to him and mussed her bangs. "Well, there will be more eggs, don't worry. And there will be baby turtles hatching for the rest of the summer to grow into more Mother Turtles. Are you sure that's all that's making you unhappy?"

"I don't want our vacation to end. I don't want to leave the Island, Daddy. We may never see it and the ocean and Renee and Cherry and Brenda and Mr. and Mrs. Goodwillie and the Ship House again."

Daddy laughed, but it was a kind laugh. "Such a long list of discoveries! How many little girls and boys would have liked to make them, too, and in only two weeks. Try to be thankful. We'll come back sometime to see our friends. Why don't you think about that?"

Suki tried to be thankful. She tried to think about coming back to the Island sometime. She tried to sing the 'gator song. But when she went to sleep that night, the lump was still in her throat.

11

Saturday dawned clear and golden.

"A perfect day for flying," Daddy said.

"I hope it's like this in Chicago," Mother said.

After breakfast Mother packed the suitcases while Suki took a last swim with Daddy and Brenda.

Now Suki was picking up all the shells her pockets and one small paper bag would hold. She wished she could take them, each and everyone— angel wings, scallops, whelks, moon snails, olives, wedges, cockles, augers, razor clams—she had learned their names from the shell book. Lavender and yellow, black and pink, chalky white and mossy green. She wanted all of them! She was so busy she did not notice Renee and Cherry sneak up behind her.

"Boo!" Renee yelled, and Suki jumped, dropping shells in all directions.

"Oh, you scared me!" Suki laughed.

"Mrs. Goodwillie called and invited us to go along to the airport," Cherry said.

"For a send-off party," Renee added.

"My daddy says we're coming back sometime," Suki said weakly.

"Everyone comes back once they get this Island sand in their shoes." Cherry smiled her wonderful smile. "That's an old saying around here. Let me help you with the shells, Suki. How about one of each kind, wouldn't that be better than trying to take such a pile?"

59

"Probably, since Mother said *a few*."

"You don't have a sand dollar!" Renee exclaimed.

"What's a sand dollar?" Suki thought she had found every kind of shell there was on the beach.

"It's the best one of all," Renee said, running to the water's edge. "The tide is low—a good time to find them. They're kinda buried in the sand."

Crabs and sandpipers were searching for food, their delicate tracks criss-crossed the packed wet sand.

"I've found one!" Renee cried.

Suki looked at the flat brown object. "I didn't know that was a shell. I've dug up lots of those, but they aren't shells, are they?"

"Sure they are," Renee said. "Fossils, Aunt Cherry calls them."

"We can tell better from the dried-out ones. See? I found these above the waterline," Cherry said. "When sand dollars are wet and alive you can't see their design too well, but look at how it shows up on these bleached ones."

Suki could not believe her eyes! A five-petaled flower was centered on the shell. Its lines were fine and perfect as though an artist had painstakingly etched them there.

"Look! There's a star in the middle of the flower," Suki said softly.

"Turn it over," Cherry urged. "There's another flower on the underside."

Sure enough, there was another flower, a larger one.

"A flower on the bottom and a flower on top. How beautiful," Suki whispered.

"Beautiful and amazing," Cherry said "The sand dollar has no head, but it has teeth. It has no gills or feet, but its hairlike spines enable it to swim around and gather food. See the slightly curved surface? That shape plus its design inside lets it move through the water without the slightest friction, just like the diving saucers used by oceanauts."

"Oceanauts?" Renee had not heard that word before.

"Yes, space explorers are called astronauts, as you both know—ocean explorers are called oceanauts."

"You're too technical, Aunt Cherry," Renee chirped. "She calls sand dollars fossils and skeletons, Suki. Imagine! To me, they're pretty shells with flowers on them. And the best part is inside—the *birds*."

"Birds?" Suki said, bewildered.

"Break the sand dollar in two."

"Oh, I don't want to spoil it, Renee."

"There are more whole ones around, Scaredy. I think the star and the birds are so, so mysterious!"

Suki could not bear to break the lovely shell in half, but now she *had* to know what was inside. It cracked down the middle like a stale cookie, and into her hands fell the star and five tiny "birds." Their wings were spread like gulls or white doves flying.

"It's magic," Suki whispered. "The sand dollar is magic! Just think—flowers on a shell and birds inside! Oh, Cherry, did God make this up too?"

"Yes, Suki, only *He could*. Out of nothing. He created everything—the birds that fly, the life in the ocean, the sun, the moon, the planets, the snowflakes, the sand dollars—only *He* could make them up."

From the Ship House the station wagon horn sounded. It was time to go to the airport. Renee picked up the bag of shells and Suki stuffed her pockets with sand dollars, the broken one and four whole ones. There would be one for each of her sisters—one for Best Friend, the Invisible Peacock—and, of course, one of her own just to keep.

The trip to the airport was, oh, so short.

Daddy checked the tickets.

Mr. Goodwillie carried in the bags.

Brenda was so excited she jumped up on perfect strangers.

Mrs. Goodwillie and Mother talked about "next summer."

And Suki held hands with her friends, Renee and Cherry, until it was time to say good-bye.

"If you're ever in Chicago, come to see us," Daddy said, handing one of his business cards to Mr. Goodwillie and one to Cherry. "You'll be welcome anytime."

"Flight 426 now boarding," the voice over the loudspeaker announced.

Once more Suki took a seat by a window.

Mother and Daddy sat behind her.

The "bluebird" which had been waiting silently at the gate now took a big breath, and its engines exploded into a roar. After the little plane taxied away from the gate, it sped along the runway, faster and faster.

Slowly it lifted and they were airborne.

It had all been real.

And magic too.

Joyce Blackburn has written fifteen published books since leaving a professional career in Chicago radio. Her recording of *Suki and the Invisible Peacock* led to a contract for her first book of the same title. Subsequent prize-winning titles for young readers have made Blackburn well-known among librarians and teachers. She has also gained recognition in the field of popular historical biography and enjoys an enthusiastic adult following. Blackburn, a resident of St. Simons Island, Georgia, received the 1996 Governor's Award in the humanities from the Georgia Humanities Council. Her works are in the Special Collections of the Woodruff Library at Emory University, Atlanta, Georgia.